The Specific Ocean

Written by Kyo Maclear

Illustrated by Katty Maurey

KIDS CAN PRESS

Rocky River Public Library

Today we leave for summer vacation.
I do not want to go. I want to stay in the city
with my friends. But Papa says no, we're leaving.

At the airport, I drag my suitcase behind me.
There will be nothing to do. On board, I feel the
rumble of the plane and then we climb, up above
the busy streets and the tiny rooftops. We climb
through puffs of cloud, and the city is gone.

We are staying in a boxy house on
the Pacific Ocean. All we can see is water —
a never-ending roll of gray-blue-white. Dull,
droning, dreary water.

"What do you think?" asks my older brother.
I shrug. Then I go and count the days until we go home.

The next morning, my brother races down to the ocean. Mama nudges me to follow him, but I shake my head. I know the water will be cold. *Steal-your-breath-away* cold.

I'd rather do nothing.

boring grass

MOPING SCHEDULE

9:00 – 10:00   Watch dust

10:00 – 10:30   Play chess alone

10:30 – 11:00   Pull loose thread

11:00 – 12:00   Stare at the walls

boring
rock

boring sea

On the third day, I follow slowly, grumping down the path. The water *is* cold. Even colder than I thought. But we wade in and swim fast. We swim along the rocks. We swim through spots of warmth.

The next morning, I jump out of bed —
a flurry of bedsheets. My brother rushes to
catch up with me on the beach. We float on
our backs, and the wind blows ripples across
the water's surface, and those ripples grow
into waves that lift us up and up.

Later, we walk with the seabirds along the shoreline where the tide rolls, backward and forward, over our feet. Splish, swish, splosh, splash. The whole world rushes ahead, but the ocean does its own thing, rolling backward and forward. Wash, swash, splush, hush.

There is no late or hurry or racing in ocean time.

Here's a secret …
I used to call it the Specific Ocean
until my brother corrected me.

But he doesn't know that a place can have two
names: one that is correct and for saying out loud, and
one that is private and for saying inside your head …

When the sun comes out, we sit on the rocks
and watch the waves. Shine, shimmer, gleam, glow.
It makes me dizzy to imagine where the sea ends.
The ocean is so big that it makes every thought and
worry I have shrink and scatter.

But one thought stays:

I want this ocean to be mine.

Mama has a snowy mountain in Japan,
and Papa has the South Downs in England.

I want this ocean to be mine. I want to
put it in a bowl and carry it home to the city.
If I had my own ocean, I could let my thoughts
swim free and dream of an underwater life.

I want to put the ocean in a bowl.

But my brother (who does know some things)

says if I do that, the ocean will be less. He says

the ocean may be big, but *it isn't endless*.

I try to imagine the earth with no ocean.

Would the coasts bump together?

The bright coral reef drain of color?

The large yellow moon lose its mirror?

"How about a glassful of ocean?" I ask my brother.

He shakes his head.

So I leave the ocean as it is, for next time.

Tonight is our last night here. I do not want to go.
As the house grows quiet, I can hear it. I can hear the sound
of the waves rolling in and out, backward and forward.

I can hear the dolphins splashing and the herring jumping
and the whales singing their underwater songs. I can even
almost hear the quiet snails and sleepy starfish near the
bottom where it's too dark to see.

If people ask, I'll tell them the ocean is full of noises.
Then I'll tell them that if they listen very carefully, they
might even hear the ocean in their own breath. *Hush*.

My brother (who sometimes surprises me) says there is still so much we do not know about the ocean. The ocean is a mystery of mysteries.

But I can imagine.

I can picture every swimming thing moving from reef to reef, moving down into the deep secret places where I cannot see them, all those creatures silent and invisible. And that's when I know: I don't need to put the ocean in a bowl.

DUMBO OCTOPUS

CLOWNFISH

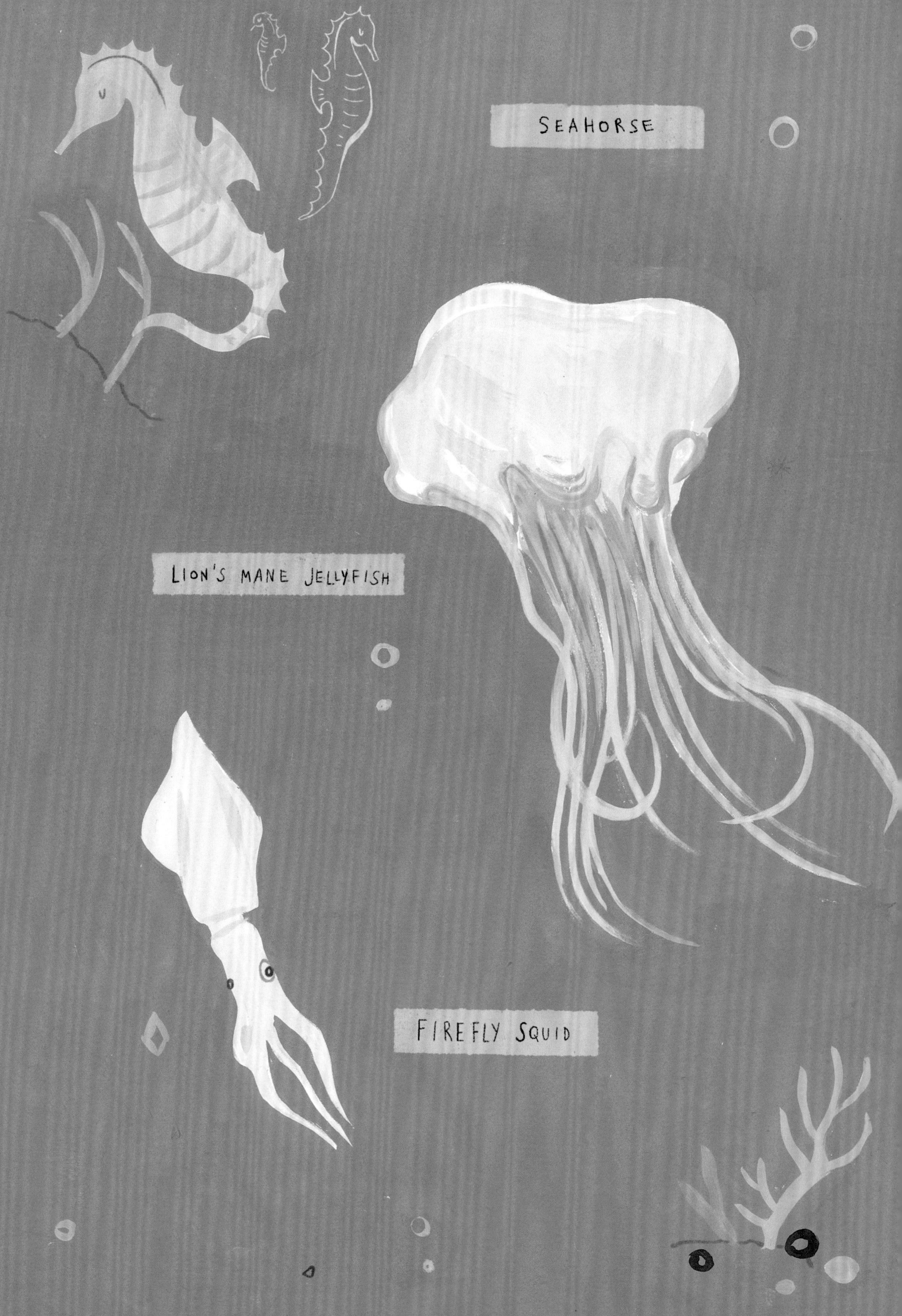

SEAHORSE

LION'S MANE JELLYFISH

FIREFLY SQUID

Because even when I go home, back to the city and my friends, it will all still be there deep down inside of me. Calm. Blue. Ruffled. Gray. Playful. Green. Mysterious. Black. Foggy. Silver. Roaring. White.

No matter where I am, this specific ocean will be with me.

For the beach boys: Toma, Mika and Yoshi.
With warmest waves to Katty, Yvette and Karen. — Kyo

To my mom and dad. 我爱你们 — Katty

Text © 2015 Kyo Maclear
Illustrations © 2015 Katty Maurey

All rights reserved. No part of this publication may be reproduced, stored in a
retrieval system or transmitted, in any form or by any means, without the prior
written permission of Kids Can Press Ltd. or, in case of photocopying or other
reprographic copying, a license from The Canadian Copyright Licensing Agency
(Access Copyright). For an Access Copyright license, visit www.accesscopyright.ca
or call toll free to 1-800-893-5777.

Kids Can Press acknowledges the financial support of the Government of Ontario,
through the Ontario Media Development Corporation's Ontario Book Initiative;
the Ontario Arts Council; the Canada Council for the Arts; and the Government
of Canada, through the CBF, for our publishing activity.

Published in Canada by
Kids Can Press Ltd.
25 Dockside Drive
Toronto, ON M5A 0B5

Published in the U.S. by
Kids Can Press Ltd.
2250 Military Road
Tonawanda, NY 14150

www.kidscanpress.com

The artwork in this book was rendered in mixed media.
The text is set in Cantoria.

Edited by Yvette Ghione
Designed by Karen Powers

This book is smyth sewn casebound.
Manufactured in Shenzhen, China, in 3/2015 by C & C Offset.

CM 15 0 9 8 7 6 5 4 3 2 1

Library and Archives Canada Cataloguing in Publication

Maclear, Kyo, 1970–, author
    The specific ocean / written by Kyo Maclear ; illustrated by Katty Maurey.

ISBN 978-1-894786-35-5 (bound)

    I. Maurey, Katty, illustrator II. Title.

PS8625.L435S64 2015   jC813'.6   C2014-906980-4

Kids Can Press is a **corus**™ Entertainment company